ANGELINE

"Unrequited Love is still Love."

By

John Charles

**Grosvenor House
Publishing Limited**

This book is published by
Grosvenor House Publishing Ltd
Link House
140 The Broadway, Tolworth, Surrey, KT6 7HT.
www.grosvenorhousepublishing.co.uk

This book is a work of fiction. Any resemblance to
people or events, past or present, is purely coincidental.

A CIP record for this book
is available from the British Library

ISBN 978-1-78623-686-9

Acknowledgments

To, N, N, C and C. You know who you are, and you know what you did. Thank you for Believing. With all my Gratitude. And Love.

PART ONE

"Unrequited Love is still Love."

Jayne.

"How is he being different?"

Good question, thought Jayne, taking another sip of her coffee before looking up at Claire, her best friend for... oh…God knew how long.

"Dunno," she said, shrugging her shoulders. "Just different."

"Oh well, that's as clear as mud." Claire smiled, unsure inside as to where this was going. Jayne was always so positive, so clear minded, but today?

There was a silence. Jayne and Claire usually enjoyed their catch up time, a once weekly chance to chill, unwind, and natter.

Jayne looked up. "Oh forget it, it's probably just me, tired." She didn't mention the specific episode that had so upset her. There didn't seem to be much point.

The talk drifted back to its usual topics, kids, gossip, and Claire's latest disastrous relationship. Safe stuff.

After a brief heartfelt hug they went their separate ways.

"I'll text you."

"You'll be fine."

"See you next week."

"Love you, bye."

Jayne joined the queue out of the retail park, turned on to the slip road and edged her way back homewards in the slow moving traffic. Her mind had time to wander. Why had she mentioned Neil to Claire? Jayne loved Claire to bits but was also aware that Claire was too wrapped up in her own imagined woes to ever consider thinking about anyone else's troubles. And besides, admitted Jayne to herself, Claire and Jaynes relationship was based partly on Jayne's ability to administer calm words and sensible advice as Claire went through yet another traumatic experience.

It was a relationship which suited both; Claire needed a shoulder to cry on, frequently, and Jayne relished the role of confidante, older sister. Jayne felt the tears well up again. She fought them back.

"Oh Neil." She said. Out loud.

Twenty four years together, twenty two as husband and wife, life partners. Two great children, never a blip. Neil had been her rock when mum died, he was a great dad, a good husband. Steady. Good. A good man. How many times had she heard that? And now, a change in him, discernible. Neil seemed a little? Well she couldn't put her finger on it, but a little distant perhaps, preoccupied? And the other night? So out of character. So not Neil.

People change, its allowed thought Jayne. People grow, change, and develop new interests. Pressure at work? No. He would have said. No secrets.

"Oh, whatever." She sighed as she reversed onto the driveway of the neat semi she called home. She dropped the shopping on to the kitchen table, kicked off her shoes and flicked the kettle on.

Minutes later, drink in hand, Jayne flopped into her armchair, glanced at her phone, and relaxed. She looked at the silver framed photograph perched on the edge of the cabinet. She loved this picture, a beach in Devon; Neil, Amy their daughter, Jack their son, and Jayne herself, all smiling, arms entwined, leaning against a pier head wall.

The picture had been taken by Ruth, Jayne's mum, God rest her, five, no six years ago. Happy, happy times.

How quickly they had grown, her children, how quickly they had matured. Jack was twenty now, away at Leeds University, a degree in Criminology in the offing. Doing so well, settled, looking more like Neil, tall, handsome, her boy. And Amy, eighteen going on thirty, heading out to Bristol, to study Psychology, so self-assured, yet so very young and vulnerable. Maybe that was what was different now? Maybe Neil, so long the centre of his children's life, and his very reason for being, was feeling left out, abandoned? God knows, Jayne thought, she was.

Jayne went upstairs for a quick shower. She had an hour before she was due to pick up Amy, who was working in a local nursery during the summer, before a three week vacation, and then her move, away. Jayne pulled on a grey baggy Nike sweatshirt and black leggings, resisting the temptation to step into a pair of skinny jeans as Amy would be wearing jeans, and Jayne, the same size, a ten, as her daughter, wouldn't feel comfy with that. Scrunching her pale blonde hair into a scruffy bun Jayne took a quick glance into the bedroom mirror. Forty two? Looks thirty, not bad. She had heard that before, and enjoyed it. She grabbed her car keys and left.

Two weeks earlier.

Angeline.

Took a deep breath, fixed a smile on her face, and marched through the door. First day, first proper day, working, following on from three days training. Intense. Rushed.

Good luck Sweetheart. A text, from mum. Nothing from anyone else. Like who? Dad maybe? But no, dad was away on business. He was working.

Melissa from H.R. smiled and rose to meet her. Melissa was attractive, well-groomed and efficient.

That'll be me one day. Thought Angeline, without conviction.

Angeline swept her black mane of hair from her face. Should have worn it up. Too late now. She followed Melissa's confident sway down the highly polished marble corridor, conscious of the clacking sound her stiletto heels made. Should've worn flats. Too late now. Melissa was talking. "Regeneration of the business… huge investment…raising our profile overseas." It tripped off the tongue lightly. Like a walking, talking brochure. Angeline heard it, this mantra, as she had heard it repeatedly for the last three days.

"And this is Neil's office." Melissa rapped on the door, and entered. Angeline stood tall, pulled in her non-existent tummy, smoothed down her black pencil skirt, and followed Melissa through the door.

Neil.

Looked up as Melissa entered. He half rose as she smilingly introduced Angeline. "Neil, this is Angeline, Hayley's replacement. Angeline, this is Neil. Neil is section head and he'll be looking after you from now on." And with that Melissa spun on her heels, smiled winningly at Angeline, and strode out.

"Hi." Neil proffered his hand.

"Hello, I'm Angeline." Angeline shook the outstretched hand, firm. Neil noticed that Angeline pronounced her name Ornjaline. The J was soft. The name, he thought, was perfectly apt.

"Yes I know...er... please sit down."

And so Angeline sat demurely as Neil enthused about the business. How it had grown exponentially after the firm had replaced steel solar glass panel frames with aluminium ridings, making them lighter and more weather resistant. With that simple, yet extremely innovative idea the company had flourished, cornering a niche market that was expanding rapidly. Neil went to great pains to explain to Angeline how important it was that the alloys used were very cost effective, easy to mass produce. This made their product an extremely attractive proposition aboard where solar panelling was being used almost exclusively in new- build.

And so to Neil's department, Overseas Marketing, and the new projects, Milan and Turin, where a mastery of the Italian language was going to be invaluable. Angeline spoke fluent Italian, her mother was from Italy, and had insisted that Angeline be able to speak in her mother tongue. Angeline had also just attained a Master's Degree in European Economic Business Studies. She was, on paper at least, the perfect replace-ment for Neil's former assistant, Hayley, who had left owing to her husband's job being transferred to Dubai. Hayley's husband worked as a systems analyst for a large petrochemical concern, and he went where the action was.

Neil was aware he was babbling, trying to make the right impression. For some reason it seemed important to him that the Company, and, although he would have been loath to admit it, he himself, were seen in their best light. He felt uncomfortable, yet elated at the same time, a mixture of feelings he didn't immediately recognize. The pep talk drew to a close, Neil showed Angeline her desk, logged her on to the system, and gave her a brief resume of her immediate duties. In the proximity of the office they would occasionally brush against each other, and even the fleeting moment when Angeline's hair touched Neil's forearm it felt to him like an electric shock.

Hayley reappeared to whisk Angeline off for a tour of the rest of the impressive building, and Neil collapsed in his chair, to collect his thoughts. Angeline was the latest in a long line of bright young things that had come to fill the position of junior trouble shooter, as Neil liked to refer to the newly invented post allocated to his department.

It was an exhausting job, which was why a few incumbents had already fallen by the wayside. Neil was really impressed by Angeline. She was intelligent, educated, asked the right questions, and quite stunningly beautiful.

That last sentence had come into his mind quite unbidden, and Neil was surprised to find that a picture of Angeline, sat opposite him, legs crossed, hands clasped together, listening intently to his diatribe, with her head cocked to one side in earnest interest, was firmly embedded in his consciousness. She looked like an Angel, a really naughty Angel. Neil's heart missed a beat. He jumped up. Coffee. Walk. Anything.

Jayne.

Helped Amy stack the dishes into the dishwasher, and then sat in the lounge with a glass of wine. Amy disappeared upstairs to her room. She would be lying on her bed, on her phone for hours, talking to God knows who, about God knows what. This is what teenagers do, apparently, thought Jayne.

Over the evening meal Jayne and Amy had discussed plans for Amy's move to Bristol, unconditional, a place, a future, waiting for her. Jayne had attempted to involve Neil in the ongoing conversations about Train timetables, duvets, sensible eating etc., but he appeared distracted, again.

"Everything okay babe?" Her opening gambit, once Amy had floated off upstairs.

Neil had looked startled for a second, and then grunted, "yeah, good."

Jayne, with a sinking feeling in her heart realized that she had nowhere to go with this. She sat back in her chair. She had no appetite for the dross on t.v. and even less for her Open University coursework. Neil appeared engrossed in a large yellow and black covered book. She glanced at the title. "Italian for Dummies".

More sodding work, thought Jayne. The silence hummed in the air.

"How's the new girl?" she asked, fishing for common ground. Neil shot her a sideways glance.

"She's er... okay. All right I guess. She'll do, I suppose."

"Oh, good, and work?"

"Bloody Hell Jayne that's the third time you've asked that. Work is fine. The new girl's fine. Everything's fine. I'm going to bed." Neil threw the book down on the couch, and walked out. Jayne watched him go.

An hour later Jayne, naked, slipped into bed. She had sat in the quiet lounge, thinking. Thinking. Was she just imagining all of this? They were soon to be without Amy, which was an awful thought. She remembered how strange and sad it had been when Jack had left, and now he was about to enter his third year, his visits home becoming less frequent, his own life affording him less reasons to return to the fold. And now Amy, their beautiful daughter, soon to be going too.

Maybe, she thought, Neil felt like Jayne, nervous. Empty.

Jayne gently kissed the nape of Neil's neck, her long blonde hair tickling over his broad, smooth shoulders. Neil stirred. Not asleep, she knew. She ran her fingers down Neil's chest and stomach, tracing lines down to his penis. She had always secretly marvelled at how, with a few deft strokes, she could bring Neil to full arousal.

Neil was a considerate lover and he always seemed to recognize her mood, how she wanted to be loved. Invariably they made love, they didn't fuck. Jayne loved the foreplay, his gentleness, his passion, always with feeling.

Jayne had been fucked, and fucked over, in the past, in her youth, a previous life, no, a previous existence, and she loved Neil for the fact that he always, always cared.

Neil abruptly turned over and pushed Jayne's arms down to her sides. Jayne, surprised, momentarily resisted and pushed back at Neil's hands. He pressed down on her with a stronger grip, and kissed her hard on the lips. Jayne opened her eyes as Neil's tongue forced its way into her mouth. Neil always kissed her with his eyes shut, always, thought Jayne. She had peeked a look so many times. But now his eyes were open, focused, staring. He pulled her legs apart, and pushed in.

Jayne let out a grunt of surprise and wrapped her long legs around Neil's waist, pushing up to meet him as he thrust into her.

If this is what it takes to get you back, she thought...

He rode her hard, rhythmically, his eyes now clenched tightly shut, his face red. Ugly. He bit her nipples, hard, and chewed on her lower lip until, in pain, she pushed his face away. He pulled her up from the bed and took her from behind. How long since? No, he had never… He came. She didn't. He turned away. Eventually he slept. She didn't. She cried silent tears, her body convulsed, confused, hurt.

Eventually, the tears racked themselves out. Neil didn't stir.

Angeline.

It was going well. She felt confident, relieved. She could relax now. A new beginning, a new start, a good job, with prospects, a chance to put her past... wait, no need to dwell. And Neil, her boss, well he was lovely. He took time to explain things, he didn't get cross when she didn't understand things immediately. He made her laugh. Yeah, Neil was a nice guy.

Walking towards the end of her road, Angeline had time to reflect, to begin to let go of the feelings which had driven her to practical solitude these last months. She could feel the knots in her stomach, but they weren't as tight, as nauseating.

Neil was sat in his car, waiting for her, as always. Three days in to her new job and she'd happened to mention the infrequency of, and crowding on, the buses she had to use to get in to work. Neil had immediately suggested that, as he passed by her road every morning he would be happy to give her a lift. Angeline had gratefully accepted. She could drive, but didn't have a car. She hated buses, and was sometimes driven to near panic when hemmed in by strangers.

Neil was always cheerful, his car had a nice smell, and he played good music. And so, only days into her second week Angeline was beginning to feel comfortable. Happy.

"Good morning Lady Penelope." This was how he greeted her now. A little in-joke. She understood that the Penelope bit came from Penelope Cruz, the actress, as Neil had said that Angeline reminded him of her. She wasn't however sure where the "Lady" bit came from. She was too embarrassed to ask.

"Bog off." She replied, in her best Northern accent. They both laughed.

"Get in or I'll go without you."

"No you wouldn't do that." She patted him gently on the shoulder as she fastened her seat belt.

"No, I wouldn't." He half murmured, to himself. He hadn't told Angeline that taking this route to work added nearly forty minutes on to his journey. It didn't seem important.

Jayne.

The day after meeting with Claire, Jayne found herself alone in her lounge. It was late afternoon and she was climbing the walls in frustration. Amy was going out with friends after work, and Claire was preparing to meet the latest "love of my life." Jayne was at a loss.

Neil appeared, on the surface at least, to be acting more like his old self, she thought. Certainly in a better frame of mind than he had been a few weeks ago. But he was spending more and more time at work, staying later, leaving home earlier.

He is working too hard, she decided. Jayne had an idea. She would go and meet Neil after work. She would surprise him, take him for a drink, a meal. A chat. They were a team. They'd been through many ups and downs together, there was nothing they couldn't work out together.

Feeling a little more positive, a little less anxious, Jayne raced upstairs, showered, put on a little make-up, straightened her naturally wavy hair, and pulled on a tight pale pink role neck sweater, the skinny jeans, and pastel pink converse.

She sprayed on a little too much "Flower Bomb." Neil's favourite, and, grabbing her car keys, headed off towards Sol- a-Panels, a good hours drive at this time of the day.

At the end of the industrial estate the large glass and chrome visage of Sol- a –Panels rose up into the sky like an alien landing craft. This was how Neil had always described it, and although Jayne didn't quite see the correlation she went along with it.

The car park was full, it was always full, so Jayne parked on a side road. It was nearly five to, he'd be out shortly. Neil was always conscientious about texting if he was going to work late, and Jayne had been checking her phone every couple of minutes. No messages. She climbed from the car and walked across the road towards the large double gates.

Angeline.

"No, its fine, really, I can get the bus." She had hoped he would offer. She had had a shit time, out of the office for most of the day, seconded to the Finance Department, full of loud, brash young guys in red ties and sharp haircuts, all showing off. One or two of them had insisted on standing too close to her, one or two remarks were near the knuckle, inappropriate.

The work was simple enough, easy to grasp, but she found herself being shown the rudiments repeatedly. Were they just having fun at the expense of the new girl, or were they a bunch of immature pervs?

Either way she had had enough for the day, and couldn't wait to get home.

Oh where is Neil when I need him? She found herself thinking. And then, to herself, need him? That's a funny thought. She headed back to her office, their office, and Neil, her knight in Ralph Lauren shirt, pale blue. He suited that colour. And he had read her mood immediately, and offered to drive her home, even though the buses at this time of day were frequent, and he would be held up on the motorway for ages. And she had accepted, with a coy flash of her brown eyes, and she had waited for the smile that always came.

And he had smiled.

"Thank you, kind sir." She had offered, as he held the office door for her.

"You're welcome m'lady." He followed her out.

Neil.

Felt anxious. Was she okay? How would she cope with the animals up there? He had seen how they had looked at her when he had escorted her upstairs to the Finance department. Why had she had to go? There were plenty of others who could have gone. She was precious. There, he'd thought it, and now he let his thoughts, his feelings take full rein. She was funny, and sexy, and vulnerable, and tough, and... and... well, just about the most beautiful woman he had ever seen.

Neil realized, and admitted to himself, that he hadn't felt like this since he had first met Jayne, his Jayne, his wife, the mother of his wonderful children. This is so wrong, he knew, he was besotted with Angeline, his mind was filled with her, he yearned to be with her, so wrong, so very wrong.

And now, as he held the office door open for her, and she smiled that wonderful smile, and glanced at him with those mesmeric eyes he felt alive, elated. His hand briefly touched her arm and he died a thousand deaths.

They swiped out.

Jayne.

Watched as people began to pile through the double doors. She peered between the railings. She had fired off a text to Neil a few seconds before, suddenly conscious of her presence. Odd, she thought, why had she thought that necessary?

Ah, there was Neil now, tall, handsome, talking to a girl with long black hair, and she was tall too. Young. Pretty thing. Jayne started forward, preparing her opening line. "Surprise" came to mind, hardly original, but still, a nice surprise.

Neil had already reached his car and was holding the passenger door open. The pretty girl was climbing in, all leg and smiles. Neil was grinning, and heading round to the driver's side.

Jayne had stopped walking towards the car, unsure, her heart raced. Should she go on? What was Neil doing? Who was this woman? Jayne felt exposed, confused. Neil's car swept away from her. She made no attempt to bring attention to herself. She didn't phone or text him. She stood in the emptying car park. After a while she went back to her car.

Neil.

"Thanks Neil. I do appreciate it. Good night."

"You're welcome young lady. See you tomorrow."
There was an awkward pause. Should she hug him?
No. She climbed out.

Angeline walked from the car. Nice man, he's sweet.
The thought flickered through her mind as she fished in
her bag for her key.

Neil sat for a minute, in the car, watching her, his heart
was racing. She really is fucking perfect, he thought.
Again. He went over in his mind the last few days.
How he had felt, talking to her, laughing with her. How
she had spoken, intelligently, wittily, with real passion,
and her laugh, throaty, a deep chuckle. Neil felt elated.
Happy.

He drove home. The diversion had added an hour to his
journey. Normally sitting in traffic drove Neil crazy,
but nowadays he accepted it with a shrug.

Angeline.

Angeline's mother was setting out the evening meal.

"Hello bambina, how was your day?"

"Hello mama, it was ok. I'm tired. Thank God for Neil."

"Ah Neil. He drove you home, yes? He seems like a very nice man."

"Yeah, he is. He really is." Replied Angeline, smiling.

Jayne.

Had gone home and had prepared the evening meal. Neil had arrived, a little after six fifty. He glanced at her as she busied herself about the kitchen. He put the kettle on.

"Good day at work?"

"So so."

"Anything new?"

"No, nothing new."

"Who was the girl in your car?"

"What?"

"The girl in your car Neil. The pretty one. Who was she?"

The seconds Neil spent floundering around for an answer lasted an eternity.

"Oh. Angeline. Yeah I gave her a lift home. She doesn't drive. And wasn't feeling well." He trailed off, not meeting Jayne's eye. More seconds passed. Finally the question came. He cleared his throat. Looked up at her.

"Why? Did you see us? Me?"

"I came to your work, to take you out, a bit of company. You already had some." Jayne could feel it coming now. She fought it back.

"You should have rang. I would have made other arrangements for her. For Angeline."

"I did fucking ring. You were too busy playing at being a fucking ambulance. What is going on Neil?" Jayne was standing in front of Neil now, red faced. Angry. Tears were welling up in her eyes.

"What do you mean? There is nothing going on. What do you mean?"

"Neil, you're lying. I know you, I know you. There is something. Is it her? For God's sake Neil she's a girl, a young girl."

Neil, on the defensive now. "Yeah, exactly, she's a young girl, she just needed a lift home and I..."

"Stop. Please stop. Neil, I'm your wife." The word stabbed into Neil's heart. Jayne was quiet now, in control of herself. She looked steadily at him, at her husband. At the man she had loved all her adult life. "Just tell me Neil. Just tell me." Neil stood with his head down, for a long time. When he looked up there were tears in his eyes, in his heart.

"I love her Jayne. I love Angeline. I'm so sorry. I love her." It came out in a whisper. She froze. He continued;

"I didn't want it to happen. Jayne you must under..."

"Fuck you Neil. Fuck you." Jayne was in his face now, staring up at him. Shouting. "You love her? You fucking love her? You've lost your mind. You mean you fancy her. Or you've fucked her. Is that it Neil? Did it make you feel good? You disgust me. How old is she Neil? Jacks age? Amy's age?" Jayne was sobbing now, near to hysteria. She backed away from him. Neil moved forward, unsure

"Get away from me. Get out. Get out of my house. Get out." She shouted at him. Screamed at him. Until he left.

Angeline.

Yeah, sure, see u then Xx. Angeline had been surprised to get a text from Neil. It had read; hey, can you meet me at the corner of your road at 7.30?

"Just popping out for a minute, mama."

"Okay baby, take care." Shouted her mother, from the kitchen.

It was a lovely summer evening, the sun was just dipping behind the trees as she walked past the closely trimmed hedges of the quiet cul-de-sac.

I wonder what I've done that can't wait till tomorrow? A thin, nervous smile etched around Angeline's mouth as she approached Neil's car. Neil looked up. He wasn't smiling his usual lopsided grin.

"Hi, Angeline. Thank you. Please, get in." Angeline walked round to the passenger side, and climbed in.

"Hey Neil, what's up?" So close now. He looked into her eyes. Those eyes.

"Angeline, you must know how I feel. About you I mean. About us?"

"What?"

"I've left her. Jayne. My wife. The kids. Everything. For us. For you."

Angeline panicked. "What are you saying? A joke yeah? You're joking. Neil this isn't funny. Please."

"But Angeline. I love you. Do you understand? I love you more than anything I've ever loved in my…"

"Neil. No. You can't do this. This isn't fair. You're my friend." Angeline, inches away from Neil, felt enclosed, trapped. A feeling she recognized.

"Angeline, we could make it work. You can't say you don't feel anything for me. I won't believe you. Angeline. Please." Neil was staring at her, imploring.

Angeline reached for the door handle. "Please Neil stop. I have to go. You can't do this. I don't feel like that about you. You're a nice guy, you really are, but Neil, no. Please." Angeline quickly climbed from the car, closing her ears to Neil's pleas. This wasn't right. This was not how it was meant to be. What was he saying? She was shocked. In shock. Angeline walked swiftly away from the car.

Neil sat for a long time, staring at nothing. He turned the ignition key to drive away, and then realized he had nowhere to go.

PART TWO

Requite.

Angeline.

Went straight to her room, ignoring her mother's call from the kitchen.

"Hey bambina, you okay?"

Angeline threw herself down on her bed, face in the pillow, and lay still for a long time. Her phone pulsed. A text. Angeline grimaced. "Oh, fuck off. Not now." She glanced at it. It was Neil.

I'm so sorry.

Sorry? Sorry? What the Hell did that mean? What was he doing? What was wrong with him? Idiot. Why did he have to spoil it? A good guy, yeah, a good listener. A kind man, like a dad at work. Yeah a work dad. But no, he was supposed to be... different.

Angeline threw the phone down on the bed, unanswered. She took a deep breath, sat up, and took a long look at herself in her dressing table mirror. Her hair was tousled, her eye liner streaked down her cheeks, and her eyes shone like black diamonds, laden as they were with tears.

Angeline knew she was what men, and women, perceived as beautiful. She had been told that, like a mantra, from early childhood. It appeared to her that her beauty was her only attribute, her only worth.

No one ever said she was kind, or intelligent. Only beautiful.

She, of course, could only see the imperfections. Her ears, she thought, were too small, the lobes couldn't carry a large earring. Her neck? Too long. She didn't wear a necklace, or choker.

Angeline could run off a whole litany of these obvious (to her) imperfections, but didn't. People, she found, were wary around her when the conversation drifted in that direction. She assumed that they thought she was being disingenuous, or seeking out compliments. She wasn't. But recently she had stopped being so hard on herself, it was one less worry.

Angeline started to run a brush through her hair, and her mind went back to Neil. And the situation. Men, she found, fell in love with her. Men, not boys. She frightened boys. Boys, to Angeline's mind were young immature guys that did her head in. So she would brush them away. There were a lot of them... Men flocked to her, charmed her, promised the Earth, but after using her to prop up their egos, or cocks, dropped her. She had had several disastrous liaisons recently, and had grown weary, and wary.

She was, in her own eyes, an easy lay, gullible, trusting, looking for ...what?

Behind the beauty and the haughty façade was a young inexperienced and lonely girl, which was why she would seek out someone to listen to her, someone she could trust, confide in. Neil had listened, hadn't judged, had smiled in recognition of her feelings, and had even expressed some of his own doubts, misgivings, and fears. And now he too had let her down.

A knock at the door. "Not now mama, not now."

"Angelica, let me in." It was her father.

"Dad!" Angeline jumped from her bed, pulled the bedroom door open and flung herself into her father's outstretched arms.

"Oh dad, dad, you're home!" Peter Coleman wrapped himself around his daughter. His only child. He was back from work. Always bloody work.

They hugged each other for ever, and then Peter, disentangling himself, said;

"Right, Angel, come downstairs and tell me what I've missed. How are you? How's the job going? C'mon, get a move on. I'm famished."

Dad would make it better. She wouldn't tell him everything, obviously, but he was here now, strong, and dark, and solemn, except with her, his Angel. Why couldn't all guys be like dad? Angeline forgot about Neil, for a while.

Neil.

Sat in his car. "Shit." He said out loud, to no one in particular, to the world. And then "Shit" again, louder. Questions reeled around in his head, what had he done? He knew how he felt, knew beyond any doubt how he felt about Angeline, about how he was totally in love with her, "yeah, you cynical bastard, this is how you feel." He had found himself saying. But now what? He had burned his bridges. He did not have a plan B. There was a thought troubling in the back of his mind. "How could he hurt Jayne so?"

Angeline.

Sat next to dad on the sofa, squeezing his arm. She felt safe, happy. But for the first, no, second time, felt uneasy.

Peter Coleman loved his daughter, his only child. He would have liked for her to have had a sister, or brother. But it was not to be. His beautiful wife, Maria, had suffered such a traumatic experience whilst giving birth to Angeline that she had vowed never again. So Peter counted his blessings, and poured all his love into his wife, and Angeline, or Angel, as he had always, always called her.

Peter worked away, too many hours, too many weeks, but it was his job.

He had worked damned hard to get where he was, and he was good at it. And, he reminded himself frequently, it provided his family with a life style that he himself, having been dragged up on a council estate in south Manchester so many years ago, could never have dreamed of.

When Peter was alone, in his car, driving the never ending motorway miles from one grey city to the next, he would sometimes let his mind drift back to the sheer desperation of his upbringing, to the soulless poverty, to the mindless incessant violence, to the sense of death before life, and he would shed an involuntary tear. Then move on.

After leaving school without any qualifications, and seemingly little future, he had been put on the treadmill. He had worked and worked, mind numbing, repetitive jobs, but he had a focus, a plan. He attended night school, adult learning, small business courses, one after the other, until the qualifications began to materialize, the jobs became more office based, more responsible. Within six years he had joined a firm of independent estate brokers, who bought, renovated and sold real estate, derelict land and disused buildings.

Peter thrived in this environment, he understood the language of the tradesmen, the builders, the craftspeople, and also demonstrated the business acumen needed to recognize good deals, maximize profit. It was a unique skill set, and the business partners, anxious to retain his services, quickly invented a post for Peter. "Head of Marketing deployment and Strategy." The title looked impressive, the financial rewards were in line with the title, and the work load was immense.

Peter worked even harder, met Maria whilst on holiday abroad, in Siena, in the heart of the Tuscany region of central Italy. He fell deeply and madly in love with this tall, elegant, dark girl. She was a waitress at one of the exquisite restaurants in the Piazza del campo. He had proposed to her after two days. She had accepted immediately, and they had married, in June, in England, a year later. They were blessed with a daughter, a year after that. When Angeline finally arrived, a whole six pounds in weight, Peter had wept uncontrollably. In truth he had never known emotion like it. He had taken his new born, this tiny bundle of cheeks, and fine wisps of black hair, to the window in the maternity suite. He had raised the blinds so he could see the stars, and promised her the Earth, and all its attendant glories. She had held his look for a second, and then settled in his arms. When it came to naming the baby, Peter was firm. Maria had wanted to call her Angelina. Peter insisted that Angeline Maria sounded better, sounded right. Maria had finally relented, and kissed her baby's forehead. Peter was promoted again, overseeing the whole of the North West of England, and with the promotion, a chance to delegate. It was still hard graft, he still had to put the miles in, but at least he had chance to see the rewards, for the company, and his family. He bought a house, a large detached new build on the fringes of Wilmslow in Cheshire.

The School Angeline attended, Alterley School for girls, was a fee paying private school which provided his daughter with the accepted social norms of her peer group, and a decent education. Peter watched his daughter grow, in an environment he had never known, could only have ever aspired to...

Peter Coleman became the man he had always wanted to be.

"Angeline, put your father down, it's time for dinner. Come now, the pair of you. Eat." Maria, so proud, so Italian. This was her time. Her man was home. Peter and Angeline laughed. Angeline held her father's hand as they went into the dining room.

My Angel is sad, thought Peter. She is sad, again. But not like before...

Surely not like the last time.

Jayne.

Felt numb. Nothing, except a pain, an ache, in the pit of her stomach, and in her heart. She couldn't, wouldn't physically move. She sat in her favourite armchair, in the house she used to call home. Looking at her favourite picture.

Now, empty. The tears had come and gone, convulsed, dried to her cheeks, chin, and neck. She had been right, she had sensed it all along, and that night when they had, when he had... She had known then. Of course she had.

Her Neil, and that fucking, whatever her name was. Bitch.

He loved her. He had actually said he fucking loved her. Jayne felt sick, again. She glanced at her phone but there was no one in the world she wanted to speak to, even if she had known what to say.

She looked again at the picture.

Angeline.

Felt her phone pulse. She ignored it, lay back on her bed. She had loved having dad home. He made such a fuss over her. She loved him so much. But he couldn't help her this time. She could hardly tell him. How could she? Nothing to tell really. She hadn't done anything. She was just caught up in? The phone pulsed again. Neil's name flashed up. She answered.

"What?"

"Angeline it's me, Neil."

"Do tell. What do you want?"

"Angeline please. I need to explain. I need to see you."

"Not a chance. Leave me alone."

"Angeline. Please." His voice was cracking, imploring.

"Jesus Neil. Where are you?"

"Bottom of your road, I've been driving." He hadn't. He had been sat in the car, unmoving, for hours.

"Right, I'll be there in five. Get this sorted. Jesus Neil, I don't need this in my life." Angeline grabbed her fleece and ran downstairs.

Neil.

Waited, anxiously. His heart was racing. He would explain. She would understand. Angeline appeared, out of breath. Angry.

"Well?" She demanded.

"Angeline... I...really didn't want this to happen... I love you and..."

The look in her eyes stopped him in his tracks. "Not good enough Neil. Do you think you might have mentioned it to me? Just in passing?"

"Angeline I'm sorry. I thought you could tell. Isn't it obvious? I haven't slept. I spend the whole time thinking about you. I've left my wife. I've left Jayne."

Angeline froze, staring ahead. "Right. Stop. I don't want to hear anymore. Neil, if your wife has kicked you out that's your problem. Neil after all I've told you, after all we've talked about, and you come to me with this. How could you? You are supposed to be my friend."

Angeline could feel a hole opening in front of her, a chasm which she knew she couldn't fall into, again.

"Angeline, I could make this right. Just give me a chance."

"What? By wrecking my life? No thanks Neil it's already been done." Angeline caught herself falling, and grasped at straws. "Neil you are a nice guy, you really are, but seriously?" She let the question hang in the air.

"Well I won't go back to her, not now." On impulse Neil reached out towards Angeline. She was out of the car in seconds, slamming the door behind her.

Jayne.

Heard the front door open and close. Neil walked into the lounge. He looked at her, and spoke, quietly. "I've just come for some things."

"Get out."

"Look Jayne I don't wanna..."

"What? Argue? Grow up? Get caught? Neil please get out. I don't want you here. Do you understand?"

"Yes I'm going. I just need to get a few things for work and..."

"Oh, so you've got somewhere to go have you? A nice little nest for you and your tart? A nursery somewhere?"

"Oh please Jayne. For fucks sake."

And so the hateful, spiteful bickering continued. Neil eventually went upstairs. Doors and drawers were banged, ransacked. Emptied.

Jayne sat, curled, in her armchair, silent, brooding.

Neil came downstairs, a suitcase and a sports bag. Full.

He stood at the front door, hesitant. Jayne stood, and made her way to the door, looking at him. Through him.

"Jayne I…"

"Get out you bastard."

"Jayne, what if I said I would never see her again?" Where had that come from?

"Oh yeah, that would help." The sarcasm dripped from Jaynes lips.

"I mean it. I know what I've lost." He hadn't meant to say any of this.

"Do you really Neil? Do you really?"

"Of course. You, and the kids. Everything."

"But you love her Neil. You love your little schoolgirl. What the fuck Neil?"

Neil looked at Jayne. At the pain he had caused, and left.

Neil.

The next week cast an eternity. Angeline transferred to the Planning and Implementation Department, citing a wish to; "develop my overall knowledge and perspective of this great company." A few eyebrows were raised, but as it had been pointed out before, the workload in Overseas Marketing was immense, and didn't suit everyone.

Neil had already accepted a long, long phone call from a tearful and angry Angeline ("who, no, wouldn't meet him again, thanks.")

She had told him that she had decided to leave the company, as soon as she had found another job to go to. She was convinced, rightly or wrongly, that tongues were wagging. Neil had panicked. He wanted to say so much, to try and convince her to stay. He offered to resign so that she could continue. "She was," he offered, "excellent at her job, and he could recommend her to any department that she fancied." She had snorted a short sardonic laugh at that.

She had finally conceded that it made sense for her to glean whatever she could from the company whilst she found somewhere else. With Neil's glowing recommendation Angeline was soon ensconced in the large, loud and brash open space of "Planning" on the third floor.

Outwardly she was friendly and involved, but inside her stomach churned, and thanks to public transport, and her own surfacing anxieties, she was a few minutes late on one or two occasions.

Neil, meanwhile, was going to pieces. The work became an irritable grind, and the relationship with Jayne was so bitter and fraught with anger and pain that he hardly ever went home, preferring to spend his evenings at a Travelodge at the end of the world. He rarely smiled, had no appetite, and found himself drinking a little too much, most nights. Not that he actually cared.

Neil thought about his children, constantly, and took some scant solace in the fact that they were both away on sabbaticals for the summer. They were, as far as he knew, blissfully unaware of the events unravelling at home.

Two weeks passed. The world, surprisingly, continued to revolve.

The new girl, Lauren, was blonde, bubbly and efficient. She was also totally besotted with Neil, who in turn, barely noticed her. He mouthed the same old platitudes, listened patiently when she explained for the umpteenth time why she didn't understand a particular aspect of the work, and didn't seem unperturbed when she insisted on sitting a little too close to him whenever she could. She thought he was wonderful, kind, handsome and protective.

In truth he was going through the motions, he could do this standing on his head. It was part of the job. Bedding the new girl in. Unfortunate turn of phrase, that.

"I'm just off to the photocopier." He announced.

"I'll go if you want." She had answered, practically falling out of her chair, smoothing down the front of her slightly too short grey skirt.

"No thanks, Lauren, I could do with a stretch." He smiled that easy, vacant smile, and left.

Lauren wondered if she was attractive to him? Maybe he didn't like younger women?

Up a short flight of stairs to the next level, and down a short corridor to the print room. Neil saw Angeline leaning against the wall outside of the print room. She was chatting abstractedly to two of the junior managers, smart suits, smart haircuts, and smart lines in chat.

Neil froze momentarily. Angeline glanced up, meeting him eyes for a second. She tossed her mane of hair with a flick of her neck and a ruffle of her fingers, and laughed loudly at some remark. Neil took a deep breath and walked towards the door. Angeline became animated, flashing her eyes at her two admirers, and giggling whilst holding her hand against her mouth.

"Is this the queue?" He asked, to no one in particular. No one answered. Angeline glanced at him, and nonchalantly pushed the door open, and held it with her arm.

"It's empty." She said. To no one in particular.

"Ah, right, thanks." As he stepped forward Neil's hand touched Angeline's outstretched arm. The touch was electric. He could barely breathe.

He closed the door behind him. He could sense her, smell her. Inside he raged.

Later, at the place he used to call home, Neil had showered, packed a few items, and then, on a whim, had prepared a meal. He had to speak to Jayne. To move things on.

Jayne had duly arrived, looking surprised to see him. She was silent, baleful.

"Lasagne, salad. I've made it."

"Whatever."

"Jayne. We have to talk. "

"Not now Neil. Not now." Jayne turned away, removing her jacket, leather, biker style, pink. Not something she would normally have bought.

"Jayne please. Sit down. We can sort this out."

She turned towards him, inches from him. Forever from him.

"Neil you've got to leave. I've told the children. It's the end Neil."

For a few seconds Neil didn't respond. Finally, in a voice trembling, a voice he barely recognized as his, a voice of anger and indignation, and deep deep fear, he said;

"Jayne, I haven't done anything. Anything. I will call Jack, and Amy, and explain. How could you? Without..." His voice cracked now. Jayne looked evenly at Neil, and then walked away from him. Towards the kitchen.

Neil stood for a while, and then walked out of the door.

Angeline.

Looked in the mirror. "Well. That was clever, wasn't it?"

She had not seen Neil for several days, well three actually, but who was counting? Until this morning, at the bloody photocopy room. She had made a bloody fool of herself with those two prats. Why?

She was so angry at Neil. She so much wanted to forget about him. To move on. But she had so much she wanted to say. To ask him. To make him know how she felt inside. He was a prat too.

She had gone out on Saturday evening, with her two closest (only?) friends. Natalie and Saffron, both of whom she had known since school. She had made an effort, heels, eyes, and a tight tight powder blue mini dress. "Come and get it, creeps." Just this side of slut.

Vodka, jaeger bombs, more vodka. It had been a disaster. Several hours of being pawed, leered at and verbally abused by horrible drunken young, and some not so young, men, and even on one occasion being spat at by a large tattooed red headed woman with a skirt around her waist, and Angeline had had enough. She sat in a corner of a loud dark night club, nursing a glass of water while her friends pointed out one "hunk" after another.

Natalie and Saffron were well aware that Angeline was a man –magnet, and were determined to hold onto her. Angeline had visibly shrunk away from the shaven headed, be-muscled louts that appeared to be her friend's definition of "fit," seeing no attraction in too-tight designer shirts, sweet, overpowering cologne, and cocky attitudes. In a last desperate measure to enjoy themselves, or 'pull', the three young women had moved on to the "Pit." The Pit was a student haunt where beer arrived in plastic glasses, and music was deafening indie.

In their figure hugging dresses the three friends stood out like sore thumbs, and they soon attracted a host of male attention.

Angeline had appeared even more horrified at the bearded scruffy "stoners," with their insipid chat- up lines, and overly sincere compliments. She decided that it was time to cut and run. She had no wish to be a convenient sperm receptacle for any of these losers. She ordered an Uber, and left Natalie and Saffron, drunk and indignant, to their quest for love.

Back home, in bed, Angeline allowed herself to think about "him". It still hurt, but time was taking its toll. And pain and memories were finally beginning to blur the edges. University, second year, the local bar, and she had spotted him. Tall, but not excessively so, slim but toned, short dark hair, nice eyes. Not really her type. She didn't really have a type but she tended to quite like the long haired Latin look. Not that she'd ever had a boyfriend, as such.

Her looks tended to frighten boys away, and the ones who did come onto her tended to be vain jerks.

She had accidentally bumped into him, at every opportunity, and after a while he would notice her, and smile. A wonderful open smile, confident, but not arrogant. She had fallen totally in love with him, and hadn't even spoken to him, yet.

In a park adjacent to the Uni, he had approached her, respectful, funny, a bit flirty, but shy too. Within weeks they were an item. He would walk her to lectures, sit with her in the library, insist on seeing she got back to her rooms. She happily (and noisily) gave away her virginity to him. She had wept a little. He had been concerned, but her tears were of joy.

He was a good lover, patient, caring, and she had grown into herself sexually, becoming more comfortable with certain aspects of their love making, and confident enough to discard anything she didn't like. This is how it should be, always. She had found herself thinking this, frequently. And then he was gone.

A note, under her door. "Too deep for me. Sorry." There was no answer to her texts, or frantic phone calls. His flat mate said that he had moved out, but she had seen him entering and leaving the apartment.

Over the next few days she tried in vain to find him, to reach him. She felt betrayed. Mystified. Suicidal.

And then the stories began to come out. He had shared all of their most intimate moments with his friends. Social media was awash with lurid accounts of how he had taken her, wherever, whenever he wanted. How easy she had been. How gullible. How dirty.

Of course he hadn't named her, but she knew. Everybody knew. And the pictures, no head, just body. Her body. He had coaxed her into sending these shots, and she had willingly obliged, dangerous, exciting.

She had fled home. Why? Why would he, could he do this to her?

It had taken Angeline a year to return to further education. A different University. No friends. No dating. She preferred it this way. It was the only way she could have managed to survive.

Even now she could not bring herself to utter his name.

Enough. She picked up her phone.

Neil.

Was sat in his car. Everything, everything was gone. Jayne, the kids, and he may as well admit it, he thought, Angeline. The façade at work was slipping, wouldn't last. He wasn't sleeping, couldn't concentrate. Didn't care. His phone bleeped. Angeline. He grabbed the phone off the passenger seat.

"Hello Angeline?"

"Are you free now?"

"This afternoon, later? Yeah, can be…"

"No. Now. I want to see you now. Or not at all."

Neil had a very important meeting that afternoon.

"Yes of course. Shall I pick you up?"

"No. I've got my dad's car. Somewhere away from here."

Neil thought fast, desperate to hold on to this chance. To her.

"What about the Belfry?" There was silence for a second.

"Yes, okay. Twenty minutes."

"Angeline, I don't think I can make it there in twenty…"

"Twenty minutes Neil, or don't bother at all." The phone went silent.

Neil rang work. He was sorry, family emergency. No it would be okay. Just pass on my apologies. Thanks. The Belfry was a good half hour away. Neil slammed into first gear, and for the first time in his life felt the rear of his car slide sideways as, with a screech of tyres he shot away from the side road, heading towards who knew what.

The Belfry was magnificent, and it knew it. Situated on the picturesque banks of the river Bollin, it had once been the stately mansion of the Berwick Family, owners of several cotton mills during the height of the blossoming industrial revolution. As befitted the grandeur and opulence of the family's fortune, Berwick Manor, as it was then known, boasted a dozen bedrooms, an enormous banqueting hall, several receptions, and countless acres of exquisitely landscaped and manicured gardens.

Following the collapse of the family's wealth in the nineteen thirties, due mainly to unwise financial dabbling, the estate had gone into debt. It was eventually stripped of most of its finery, and was used as a hospital for recuperating military personnel during, and after, the Second World War. Visiting a wounded relative, an entrepreneur by the name of Richard Myers had been astounded to find that the whole estate was up for sale.

Money was tight after the War, and the sheer cost of restoration, and the ongoing expense of the upkeep, put any prospective interested parties off. Seizing the opportunity Myers bought the estate, lock stock and barrel for a derisory sum, and then spent the best part of a decade transforming Berwick Manor into "The Retreat." A palatial Health spa, replete with swimming pools, gymnasia, healthy eating restaurants, massage and yoga sessions, etc. to serve the needs of the growing class of idle rich.

The Retreat soon became de rigeur amongst the affluent, and its ethos rode the crest of the wave of the burgeoning Health fads of the seventies and eighties. Years later Myers, now an old, and very rich man, sold the property to a southern based business consortium who changed the management, and the name. The Belfry was born. The most luxurious Hotel in the region. And the most expensive.

This last twenty months however, had seen a small but significant decrease in profits at the Belfry, and the management had decided to go all out to rectify this worrying blip. "The Twenty fifth year Anniversary Celebration." A clever strategy to utilize and maximise the use of all the Hotel's facilities, especially in the quieter periods.

As the Belfry was just visible from the motorway Neil and Angeline traversed on their way to work, conversation had occasionally drifted as to what it would be like to visit, or stay there. Angeline had imagined four

poster beds, chandeliers and complimentary champagne. Neil had laughed, but she wasn't far off the
mark.

And now they were meeting here. They arrived at the
car park at the same instant. Neil motioned for her to
take the empty space, she stared at him and then drove
past and parked at a spot several yards further on.

As they alighted from their cars it began to spit rain.
Neil removed his jacket, and walking slowly towards
Angeline, proffered it. Angeline could have easily pulled
her own jacket from her car, but instead allowed Neil to
slip his jacket over her slender shoulders. As she was
wearing a sleeveless black vest his hand touched her
shoulder for the briefest second.

They walked in silence from the car park, and towards
the gently meandering river. Beautiful, so very beautiful,
a thought, Neil's, looking at Angeline.

Alongside the river banks nestled the heavily timbered
restaurant. The pristine white of the tablecloths floated
in a gentle breeze like cotton clouds. There was already
a fair smattering of people sat, in couples or small
groups. The quiet of conversation drifted towards Neil
and Angeline. At the pillared bar, which acted as a
sentry to the entrance of the restaurant, a young man,
fresh and groomed in a black suit and tie, enquired?

"Good afternoon, sir, madam. Are you wishing to dine
with us?"

In all honesty Neil hadn't thought that far forward. In the back of his mind he had had the idea of a drink, but?

"Yes, a table for two please." Angeline had enjoyed Neil's discomfort, and now took charge.

"Certainly madam. A table by the river, or inside?"

Neil again looked confused. This time she didn't help him.

"By the river, yes?" He faltered, looking at Angeline.

"Whatever Neil. Whatever."

The young man showed them to their table, and Neil noticed that he was having difficulty taking his eyes off Angeline. Fair enough, he thought to himself. She is beautiful.

With this thought Neil felt a little lightened. "Well I finally got you here." He offered with a smile.

Angeline glanced up, and then went back to the menu. At another table a couple were laughing, intimate. Music wafted across the restaurant, Booker T and the M.G.s were lamenting "To love somebody."

"The way I love you." In Neil's head the world was exploding.

The young man appeared, deferential, persistent.

"I hope this table is to your satisfaction sir, madam? My name is Thomas and I will be happy to wait on you today. This is our lunchtime menu, and of course we have catered for every dietary requirements. If you would like to…"

"A Bottle of wine. Red. Not German." Angeline, gazing up at the young man. "Please."

"Certainly madam."

And with the stiffest of flourishes, he was gone.

"Your dad's car is nice, a merc." Neil, drowning in self-doubt.

"Yes I know. I drove it."

There was silence. The waiter arrived with the wine. Without looking at Angeline he poured a quantity into Neil's glass. And stood.

Neil lifted the glass and solemnly handed it over to Angeline, who sipped it and put it down, with the faintest hint of a smile. Thomas filled the other, empty glass, left the bottle next to Neil, and, with a quiet "Thank you. Enjoy your wine," was gone. Neil chose this moment.

"Angeline, I'm so glad that you want to talk. There is so much I want to say."

"Neil let's just eat. I don't know why I'm here. I need time to think. This could be a mistake."

Neil opened his mouth just as the waiter arrived, again.

"Is the wine satisfactory sir, madam? Excellent. Would you care to order now or would you like a little more time to peruse our menu?"

"Prawn salad, wholemeal roll, and some iced water with a slice of lemon, please." Angeline, assertive.

"Thomas looked at her for a second, met her stare, and then looked away.

"Make that two." Neil, needed the space, the time. He didn't like seafood, prawns in particular.

Neil noticed that the waiter was again looking at Angeline. His blood ran cold.

Thomas spun on his heel, and was gone.

Angeline looked down at her lap, and Neil looked at her. Looked at her hair, cascading down over one shoulder, so soft, so black, and at her lips, bowed, the top lip raised a little, a permanent, sexy pout. Every now and then she would glance up and Neil's heart would leap. Neil knew in his heart that he had never felt like this before. Would never again.

The food arrived with a matadors flourish. Thomas had decided to show these proles just exactly how professional he was, how good at his job. Thomas didn't like the feeling he was being gently mocked. Or that these two were playing silly mind games with each other, which to Thomas, a confirmed people watcher, was quite evident. He looked again at the young woman. She was, he admitted to himself, quite beautiful.

Thomas laid out the plates, enquired if he could be of any more service? "Please, enjoy your meal." And was gone. Rod Stewart intoned "The first cut is the deepest."

The meal, delicious, was eaten in silence. Neil was transfixed even by the way she ate. Delicate, savouring every morsel. She picked at her salad with long slim painted fingers, and occasionally smiled to herself. A game? The thought flashed through Neil's mind. Dismissed. But banked.

Thomas the waiter duly arrived at the appropriate juncture. "Was everything to your satisfaction, sir, madam? Excellent. Would you like anything more, dessert or a coffee perhaps?"

I'd like to fucking stab you. Thought Neil. And stop looking at her, you prick.

"Erm... No we're fine thank you. Just the bill please." Was what actually came out of Neil's mouth.

"Certainly sir." And Thomas the waiter was gone.

"Angeline, are you ready to tell me why you asked me here? I mean..."

Angeline looked steadily at Neil. "Yeah, I need to clear a few things up. In my mind. We can walk along the river?"

Neil's heart jumped. "Yes of course we can."

Thomas appeared, hovered, and then stepped in.

"Sir, madam, your bill. And with our compliments…"

Thomas put down a small silver tray in front of Neil, studiously ignoring Angeline. On the tray, a small silver envelope. Thomas disappeared.

"What the fuck?" Neil prised the envelope open. An ornate Gold embossed sheet. He read aloud.

Dear Guest. As part of our ongoing twenty five year anniversary Celebrations we are proud and happy to offer you a stay in one of our prestige Gold plus double suites with an amazing discount! You will pay only twenty five per cent of the normal charge! There followed a long list of conditions and exclusions but in a nutshell Neil and Angeline were, apparently entitled to an afternoon or evening stay at the Belfry, at a massively reduced price, any time in the next twenty five days.

The stay included use of the pools, spa treatments and Gymnasium. These were at the same discounted rate, and were only available at what Neil considered to be off peak times. It was, however, he readily admitted to himself, still a great deal.

"Can you fuckin believe this?" He asked Angeline. She looked at him quizzically.

"Maybe you and your wife could have a nice night here?"

The look of pain on Neil's face shot into Angeline. "I'm sorry." She said. "That was uncalled for." She looked at him. At his pain.

They sat, in silence. Neil, after mild protestations from Angeline, paid the bill. He paid in cash, and left a handsome tip.

"Angeline, why did you ask me to meet you?"

"Let's walk. No. Let's go and have a look inside." That riposte left Neil dumfounded.

"The Hotel? You want to…"

"Yeah, we always used to talk about it, remember? I want to see what it looks like."

"Well, I don't know whether we can just…"

"Use that thing." She gestured at the letter. "We can say we want to choose a room. Anything. Come on Neil, you're supposed to be a salesman." And with that Angeline stood, sucked in her non-existent tummy, flicked her hair back with an over-elaborate flourish, and marched off in the direction of the Hotel.

Neil grabbed the jacket that Angeline had left draped over her chair, and followed her. Thomas watched them go. He so didn't want to be a waiter. He wanted to be rich, successful. Have a beautiful woman on his arm. Like that guy. He was surprised at the twenty pound note left as a tip on the tray. "Lucky, lucky bastard." He said, under his breath.

Neil caught up with Angeline, and they walked together up the long straight path which cut through the manicured lawns, heading away from the river, and on towards the grey granite façade of the Belfry. They mounted the three broad stone steps and entered the reception area.

"Chandelier." Whispered Angeline. Neil was completely lost. What was going on? Angeline practically skipped in, still staring in awe at the Chandelier, hovering like a twinkling gold Alien landing craft from the huge domed ceiling, which in itself reaches ever skywards towards the Heavens.

They walked across the oaken floor towards the grey and pink wall of marble which constituted the reception, and waited behind a middle aged couple, Americans, who were checking out. Angeline and Neil had time to take in the tasteful opulence around them, the sweep of the granite stairway weaving its way ever upwards towards the upper floors, the marble pillars supporting the mezzanine, and the red velvet Baroque couches lining the walls. It was, reflected Neil, quite magnificent.

The receptionist, Asian, tiny, immaculately turned out in black suit and gold tie, smiled a perfect, practised smile.

"Good afternoon. Welcome to the Belfry. How may I be of service?"

Hesitation. What exactly were they doing here? Neil thought quickly and said; "Ah, good afternoon. We have just enjoyed a delicious meal at your riverside restaurant and we were given this." Neil proffered the silver envelope.

Tai Ling, her name was emblazoned on the subtle gold pin on her jacket, smiled, glanced at the envelope, and asked; "Would you like to book one of our suites sir? We have several dates available, for days or evenings."

Neil looked completely baffled. Angeline stepped in.

"We'd like to book for tomorrow if you have a suite available? For the day."

"If you'll give me a moment to check, Madam? Ah yes, we have the Balfour suite available between ten a.m. and four thirty? Overlooking the river."

Angeline smiled sweetly at the receptionist. "That would be fine, thank you."

"Certainly madam. And of course we have a full range of exclusive Hotel and Spa facilities which you may use at our specially discounted rates should you so wish to access them." As she spoke Tai Ling was efficiently offering Neil and Angeline several brochures and handouts displaying a whole cornucopia of enticements including Wine tasting, Tennis lessons, and Beautifying makeover sessions.

Neil looked bemused as Tai Ling went through her sales routine. She concluded. "You can view all of our exclusive guest offers online, and of course book online, or through reception. All of our exclusive offers are subject to availability, and we reserve the right to offer you alternative dates." Tai Ling took a breath.

Angeline spoke. "May we see the suite?"

Neil shot her a glance. Could he get time off? What was actually going on?

Tai Ling took another breath, glanced at her computer screen, and then;

"Oh, I must apologise, the Balfour suite is presently occupied, but I would be happy to show you an adjacent suite, The Grosvenor, which is of the same prestigious grade, and would be available tomorrow."

"That would be lovely." Angeline smiled again, and looked at Neil.

He shuffled slightly. "That would be fine. Yes. Thank you."

"And what name would the suite reservation be under, please?" Tai Ling, sensing the uncomfortable atmosphere, moved the proceedings along. In truth she didn't care how many of these little trysts she had to witness as long as the rooms were filled, as long as the money continued to roll in. She was happy in her role, but wanted to progress, and this company suited her needs, for now.

"Clough." Neil jumped in, a little too quickly. Angeline continued to look at him, still smiling.

"Thank you Mr Clough, and may I take a contact number please?"

Neil gave his number, reluctantly, and declined the request to leave his e mail address. Tai Ling pressed a buzzer and a young man, blonde, slim, appeared. "Harry, would you mind showing our two guests the Grosvenor suite please?" And with that Tai Ling professionally handed over to Harry.

Harry took the suite swipe from Tai Ling, and turned, for all the world like an excited puppy, to Neil and Angeline.

"Good afternoon, would you like to follow me please?"

Neil put a step forward, and then Angeline spoke. "Actually no, its fine, we can wait till tomorrow. Thank you." And with that she marched out of the Hotel leaving a hapless Neil to apologize, and follow behind.

Neil caught up with Angeline, and quietly exploded. "What the fuck was that? What the fuck is going on?"

Angeline was at the edge of the car park. She turned towards him, her eyes blazing.

"Oh I see. You're fine to give me lifts, and buy me meals, even book into a Hotel room, but I'm not allowed to change my mind. Is that love Neil? You swearing at me if I can't handle a situation? Is it?" Angeline was trembling.

In that brief exchange everything changed. The balance of power, if there had been one, shifted imperceptibly. Neil stood, staring at her, staring at her beauty, at her anger. At her youth. And Neil was lost. He summoned up what he had left. "I'm sorry. I didn't mean to…"

Angeline looked away. Walked away. Back to dads car. The car she hated to drive. She was always so nervous about bumping it. Neil walked past her, looking down, not at her.

"Neil." Angeline, the rain dusting a fine sheen over her bare shoulders, called after him. He stopped, and looked around. Looking at her, but not at her. She tried to hold his gaze. "Tomorrow? Can we come? Here I mean. Can you get the time off? Just an hour. I'm sorry. I'm really mixed up. We should talk."

It had come out in fits and starts. She recognized her voice as a voice from her past. Her voice trailed away.

Neil shrugged his shoulders. He really didn't care at that very second. He didn't care about anything. Except her.

"Sure. I'll see you here at ten?" He couldn't muster a smile, didn't care.

"Yeah, ten. I'll see you here. Hey, look after yourself." Lame, what a thing to say. And she knew it.

There was a feeling inside Neil so alien that he could only nod, and quickly climb into his car. His heart raced, and his stomach knotted and ached. This was the Abyss, and he was about to fall headlong into it.

PART THREE

Consequence.

Jayne.

Heard the car draw up, saw the headlights through the half drawn blinds, heard the key turn in the lock, and heard Neil mutter something under his breath as he entered the hallway. She sat, in her favourite place, next to her favourite framed photo, and inside, felt her heart die.

Neil entered the lounge. He looked troubled, unnerved. He opened his mouth to speak, and then seemed to think better of it, and disappeared into the kitchen. Jayne heard the click of kettle and clank of cups as Neil prepared a drink. He re-entered the lounge.

"Would you like a cup of tea? I'm making one."

Jayne shook her head. No words would come. Yet.

Neil sat down. This was the time. "Jayne, I've been thinking, it's all I do actually, most of the time. About us."

She visibly blanched at that. Inside, he recoiled. But carried on.

"Jayne, we've been together so long, we've been through so much, too much to just throw it all away. Do you think, even just for the sake of the kids?"

He let it hang there. He wanted to say more, much more. But he didn't trust his voice, or his heart.

Jayne looked at him for a long second, judging what to say. How to say it.

"It's too late Neil. I've told Jack, and Amy. I've spoken to both of them. They know, Neil. They wanted to come back Neil, but I've told them to stay away, finish their trips. It will give you time to move out properly Neil. To go."

Neil fell headlong into the abyss.

"What did you say? What did you tell them?"

"I told them the truth Neil. In a way that wouldn't hurt them. As a mother should." She stared at him. Neil sat, looking at his hands, for a long time, seconds? Eventually he looked up, with the tears welling up behind his eyes. "Oh Jayne." Was all he could think to say. He stood up, slowly, not looking at her, and walked out.

Angeline.

Spent the evening with mum and dad. She watched them as they laughed, and touched, and smiled at each other. Her mum would occasionally lapse into her lilting Italian tongue when she would gently admonish Peter, who in turn would mimic her voice, and pretend to not understand what she was saying. And Angeline was happy. In this place, in this bubble, where nothing, no one, could hurt her.

And then dad would hug Angeline, and promise her the Earth, even though she hadn't asked for it. And he would kiss her cheek, and ask quietly if his Angel was okay. She would say "Yes of course." And he knew it wasn't. Peter had enjoyed his day off, his day at home, with his beautiful, loving wife, but had wondered why Angeline had been so keen to take his car.

"To visit a friend." She had said.

And she had come home, just before tea, looking pale and drawn, tired.

Peter tried to put it to the back of his mind, he only had another day away from work. He would spend it with his Angel. Sitting in the comfy colourful lounge, after yet another dessert, Peter asked Angeline: "Hey Angel, would you like to spend some time tomorrow with your old man?"

Angeline looked up, startled. "What?"

Peter hadn't noticed. "With me sweetheart. Would you like to spend some time with me? We could go to the mall. Or a drive out, somewhere nice." Angeline swallowed, took a second to collect her thoughts, and then answered: "Oh I'm sorry dad, I promised Natalie that we'd go out. I could ring and tell her?"

Peter fought to hide his disappointment. "No, don't be silly, really. You go out with your friend. Are you back at all? Maybe we could have a takeaway tomorrow night?"

"Of course, yes daddy that would be lovely." Angeline put her arms around Peter and squeezed him, hard.

Peter and Angeline both breathed a sigh of relief. For two completely different reasons.

Angeline rose early. For some reason she had slept well. She hadn't worried. She would sort this mess out with Neil. And move on...Inside her there was a different feeling, a feeling which made her feel uncomfortable but at the same time, curiously strong. Empowered. She hadn't got a clue as to what had been going through her mind yesterday, but seeing Neil squirm was strangely edifying.

Oh well, she thought, no matter what happens today, dad would be here tonight.

Angeline rose, showered, and then set about choosing what to wear. Although, that wasn't strictly true. At the back of her mind, since the previous afternoon, she had been conjuring up an outfit to wear at The Belfry. She slipped on a black bra, and lace hipster knickers, faded slim fit jeans, a scalloped black cotton top which left her shoulders bare, and which didn't quite reach her navel, and a pair of black leather thigh length boots.

With her hair cascading over one shoulder, and enough war paint around her eyes to start a second Sioux uprising, Angeline considered herself ready.

I look like a gypsy, a gypsy porn star, she thought.

"Good." She said to herself. She texted Neil.

Neil.

Looked at his phone. Hey, can you pick me up at 9.30 xx. Angeline.

Now what? Neil hadn't slept at all. He had gone back to his motorway hotel room, still in shock from Jayne's revelation, but couldn't rest, or think.

He had sat in the hotel bar, gazing at the multitude of grey suited businessmen, all idling, counting the hours till the next morning, the next meeting. He knew the feeling, he had done this himself. So many times. He had had a drink. Several in fact, but all this did was deaden the senses, didn't stop the pain, the confusion.

He had returned to the room. So quiet. Empty. What was he doing?

He had showered, tried to sleep, watched rubbish on the television for a while, and even contemplated turning on his laptop. But no, that was an unwritten law of Neil's. No computer outside of work hours.

He had risen at five fifty, thought again about phoning Jayne, and dismissed the idea. He had gone through the motions, shave, shower, dressed. He was running out of clean clothes…Didn't care. He had joined the queue for breakfast, and had eaten without appetite, without enthusiasm. And then, out of nowhere, the text.

Another game? Wondered Neil. And then, to himself, Game? Was this a game? Why did he feel that? Think that?

He returned to his room. Neil sat on the edge of the bed, looking in the mirror. He looked awful. He pulled off the jeans and grey sweatshirt, and managed to find a clean shirt, pale blue, Ralph Lauren. It could have done with an iron, but? He quickly slipped on his navy single breasted suit, brown shoes and belt, decided against a tie, and looked again in the mirror...Better.

He could at least look the part. He always felt like he could go into battle dressed like this. Felt like an equal. Not quite as inferior.

Neil gathered up his keys, wallet and phone. He stood in the middle of the room and texted Angeline. Sure. Where? Within seconds the reply came, Usual. 9.30. Ta. XX

The bottom of her road. Neil then fired off several texts, apologising for his continued absence, citing an upset stomach. His meetings would be rescheduled, and his new assistant, what was her name? She could deal with the daily stuff, fend it off. Until he got back.

Neil had never had time off without just cause before. He felt like he was betraying someone. Himself? With thoughts of Jayne and Amy and Jack in his mind he left, and set off on the half hour journey to...

Angeline.

Had been waiting for his reply.

Good, she thought, no need to book a taxi. She rang in to work," Yeah, so sorry, women's troubles. Yes. I'll be sure to let you know. Thank you." In truth she couldn't have cared less.

After leaving Neil's office the job had soon become a grind. What was the point of being fluent in Italian if she never got to use it?

What was the point of her Degree when in reality all she was now doing was glorified secretarial work? She couldn't wait to move on. Anywhere.

Angeline grabbed her fringed suede shoulder bag and black leather biker jacket, and went downstairs.

"Ah bambina, you are going out, you look bellisima!"

"Thank you mama, yes I'm out today. Back tonight. Byeee!" Angeline wanted to avoid her father. She felt? She wasn't sure. Embarrassed? Why?

She glanced at herself in the hallway mirror. "Come on then." She said to herself. "Ciao mama." She called.

Jayne.

Picked up the phone for the umpteenth time, and put it down again. She needed to call someone. Anyone. But she couldn't breathe. Couldn't focus.

Neil.

Was going to be late.

The traffic, surprise surprise, was awful. He had put his phone in his jacket, and his jacket on the rear seat of the car. Leaning back, he could not quite reach it. He thought about pulling over, but decided against it. A few minutes wouldn't make that much difference, surely? At last he pulled off the slipway, down the main road, and a sharp right onto the road which led towards Angeline. He saw her at the end of the road.

She looks like a hooker, he thought, and then she disappeared in a cloud of white smoke. E cigarette? He didn't know she smoked.

He drew up alongside her, and resisted the temptation to ask her how much she charged. "Gallows humour," he uttered under his breath.

She was stunning. And she knew it. But, a bit obvious?

Neil dismissed the thought as he got out of the car and went around to the passenger side. He held the door open, and Angeline, with the merest hint of a smile, brushed past him and slid in. The faintest touch of their bodies wasn't lost on either of them.

"Thank you." She said. Smiling up at him, sweetly.

"You're welcome, m' lady" he smiled back.

Neil climbed behind the steering wheel and turned the engine on.

"Good morning" he said. "I didn't know you vaped."

"There's probably a lot you don't know about me." It was an answer.

And with that Angeline looked down at her phone, and then out of the window. Neil pulled away from the pavement, and they drove. In silence.

Peter Coleman had enjoyed his walk. He had walked the whole perimeter of the leafy, refined Estate he was so proud to belong to. He had noticed the lack of litter, or glass, or dog excrement on the ground, the absence of graffiti on the walls, the sheer greenness of this place he called home. He always noticed these things. He never tired of noticing these things. And he could breathe. He could let it all fall behind him.

As he rounded the bend onto Wordsworth Lane he noticed, on the periphery of his mind, the midnight blue BMW as it swept past him. He paid it no heed. His mind was on other things, the past. And the present.

Neil noticed Angeline's brief look of alarm, but as he opened his mouth to ask what was wrong, she spoke.

"How long will it take to get there?" Unnecessary, but it diverted his question.

"Hmmm twenty minutes, I think. Why?"

"Just asking, she replied." She lapsed back into silence. Angeline again felt strange. Seeing her dad had brought on a second of panic. He hadn't seen her. She was a grown woman, she thought to herself. So why did she feel like this? Angeline considered asking Neil to pull over, stop, and let her out. But she didn't.

She let out a long deep breath, and watched the sun rifle through the trees. It was going to be a nice day.

Jayne.

Picked up the phone again. This feeling inside her had lasted for so long now she couldn't imagine it not being with her. Festering. Hating.

She had to talk to someone. She had considered Claire, but, in all honesty Jayne knew the response she would receive. Claire would listen, and be sympathetic, and hold Jaynes hand and then tell her that everything would be all right, it would all work out in the end. Which was why, Jayne reflected, that Claire didn't have any meaningful relationships in her life. Life, Jayne knew. Was not quite as easy as that. With the feeling growing, with her heart aching, and the wanting to run and hide growing like a cancer inside her, she gave in, and rang her daughter. No answer. She left a text.

Neil.

Parked the car, and looked at Angeline, who was pretending to look at her phone.

"Do you still want to do this?" The words came out in a falter.

"Have a look at how the other half lives? Yes, it beats work." Angeline surprised herself at how confident, assured she answered.

Neil, his head spinning, climbed out, mustered a smile, and went round to open the car door. She had waited. He loved that.

Angeline smiled as she climbed from the car, her eyes never leaving Neil's as she rose. Any misgivings Neil had felt at that moment disappeared. Angeline felt that strange sensation again. So, this is power, the thought flickered in her mind.

Jayne.

Grabbed the phone.

Amy had answered. Hey mum. The text read. Jayne considered for a second, and then texted; Hey! Hope you are having a wonderful time. Are you still in Morocco? Do you think there is any chance you could come home a few days early hun. It's the thing with your dad. It's not got any better, and I'm feeling a bit low. I will pay your plane fares if you can. If not it's not a problem. Take care my baby. All Love xx.

A large hot tear fell on to the face of the phone.

As she went to wipe it off, the phone rang.

Angeline.

Panicked inside. Now what? She walked alongside Neil up the steps of the Belfry, still in silence aside from the click of her boot heels. Should've worn flats. An echo from...when? "Too late now." She muttered under her breath as they approached the reception desk.

"Sorry, did you say something?" Neil looked concerned, nervous.

"No."

"Good morning. Welcome to the Belfry. How may I be of assistance?" Tai Ling, fresh faced, bright. Professional. She had obviously forgotten Neil and Angeline. And then, the recollection.

Angeline watched Tai Ling as she went through her routine. A confirmed people watcher, Angeline was fascinated by how faces gave away emotions, truths. Lies. Angeline decided that Tai Ling was pretty, efficient, and utterly bored by her job. Must be hard being nice to people all the time, she thought, and then dismissed her from her mind.

After a form was filled in, and yet another list of discounts proffered, accepted, Tai Ling asked Neil.

"Do you have any bags you would like taken up to your suite sir?" And then, looking at Angeline. "Madam?"

Neil and Angeline answered in unison. "No." Tai Ling continued, unabated.

"Okay, well thank you, and may I wish you a thoroughly pleasant stay." And with that Tai Ling handed over to Harry, who, it appeared, was more than happy to be of assistance.

Really? Thought Angeline. Was anybody really so polite? So happy?

As Neil and Angeline walked towards the spectacular staircase, no they wouldn't want to take the lift, Tai Ling, watching the gentle sway of Angeline's buttocks in her tight jeans thought, enjoy your intercourse, smiled, and went back to staring at the screen in front of her.

Neil.

Was also following the rhythm of Angeline's posterior as the small party ascended the stairway.

On the mezzanine, Harry veered right, uttering some inanity that neither Neil nor Angeline could quite hear. After passing three doors he stopped and gesticulated towards the huge chandelier which was now at their eye level. Neil caught "Original piece," and "restored at huge expense," but the rest was lost as Neil became aware of Angeline. She was standing close to him. She whispered "I love chandeliers." Neil was aware that Angeline spoke almost like a child. She genuinely seemed in awe of the spectacular ornate lighting hanging in front of her.

For the briefest of seconds Neil felt uncomfortable. Then he looked at her profile, and died inside.

Harry had stopped. He looked like he was about to burst such was his enthusiasm. "This," he gestured at the white door, "Is the Grosvenor Suite." If Harry noticed that Neil and Angeline were staring fixedly at the small gold plaque emblazoned with the legend "Grosvenor." which was attached to the door, at eye level, he didn't show it.

Harry swiped the fob, and they entered.

The hint of Jasmine wafted into their nostrils as they stepped into the room. Neil watched as Angeline took in the scene.

The suite was quite simply spectacular. A large circular room, almost completely white, save for a few choice gold accruement, lampshades, side table's, door handles etc., met their view. Floor length ivory coloured curtains framed a floor length window which afforded a sight of the picturesque banks of the river Bollin. The room gave way to two other rooms, a bathroom in the same tasteful style. And the bedroom.

Harry stood outside the bedroom door, about to open it.

"That will be all, thank you." Neil, anxious now, not quite sure what was to come. As Harry passed by, Neil slipped him a five pound note." Harry seemed genuinely surprised. "Thank you sir. Enjoy your stay."

"Oh, Neil how very assertive." Angeline whispered, as Harry left the room, still bowing and scraping.

"Fuck off." Neil answered with a smile which didn't quite reach his eyes. Angeline wasn't sure if she'd caught a hint of menace just under the tone of his voice. She decided to back off, a little.

Neil had stayed in a fair number of hotels in his time, but even he admitted that this was very, very nice.

"Can I see the bedroom please?" Angeline was stood next to him, imploring. Neil stepped back, and Angeline went to the door, pushed it open, and stood in the doorway."

"Is this a set up? Did you arrange this?" Angeline half smiled at Neil.

"What?" Neil stepped forward, drinking in her aroma, her warmth. Angeline didn't move from the door, so Neil leaned a little into her. His body felt, connected with, and stored in its memory bank, every last curve, contour and nuance of her very being. It felt to Neil as if he was being electrified, come to life. In the centre of the bedroom, decorated in deep plush red, and gold filigree, was a four poster bed.

"You are fucking kidding me." Neil's response.

"Oh Neil, I was right." Angeline walked up to the bed, and walked around it, running her fingers along the exquisite carved posts, and stroking the pure white silk sheeting.

Neil stood in the doorway, transfixed. Angeline seemed like a different person. Neil realised that he had no control whatsoever of this situation. He didn't care. He was with the creature who meant more to him than the whole world. Angeline toyed with the tassels holding back the bed drapes, and then abruptly said; "Right then. Let's get this sorted out." She pushed past him, back into the white circular ante room, which now, strangely, seemed smaller, less enchanting.

Angeline went to the window, looking out, framed in the glow of a white sunshine. Neil approached her. She sensed, turned, and said; "Can we order drinks?" Neil, stunned for a second, answered "Yeah, of course. What would you like?" "Champagne. I would like champagne. And some peanuts." Angeline smiled, looked at the ornate telephone sat on a gold coloured circular side table, and then sat down, gracefully, on a deep red sofa, which was nestling under the bay of a smaller, oval window.

She was now in repose, a shaft of sunlight making a halo around her face.

An Angel. A crazy, beautiful Angel. Neil had never known emotion like this. He went to the phone, dialled seven. "Bottle of Champagne please. Grosvenor Suite. Yes please, and some peanuts. Peanuts. For two? Yes. Thank you." Neil replaced the receiver, and realised he was shaking.

Jayne.

Answered immediately. "Hello baby. Are you having a good time? Lovely." Voice beginning to break, to crumble. "Oh Amy. Please can you come home?" "Oh mum of course I can. I said I'd come back. Are you all right?"

Jayne took a deep breath before answering. "Yes baby, I'm fine. Honestly. We just need to sort a few things out. Stay where you are. Really. It will be fine."

Amy could hear the tension in her mum's voice. She had tried to put her mother's last call to the back of her mind. That call to say that dad was moving out, that he and mum had fallen out, that things had changed.

Amy had wanted to come home then, but her friends had insisted she carry on with her travels. Amy had stayed with her friends, hopping train to train, country to country. But, hearing her mum in so much pain hadn't left Amy's mind. And now this. Amy decided to go back. To be with mum. "Okay mum. Whatever you think is best. If you're sure you're okay? Ring me if you change your mind. If anything happens. Okay?"

After heartfelt goodbyes they rang off. Jayne sat, in her favourite chair, looking at her favourite picture, and Amy started looking for flights back home, via her phone.

Angeline.

Really didn't know what to do. What to say. This was way out of her comfort zone, and so far she had just been testing the water, exploring. She knew she was really angry at Neil, knew that, in the space of a few weeks, her ideal job, her new start, had come and gone.

In her subconscious though, there were other questions. Why did he feel like this about her? Why had he sacrificed his marriage, even his kids for her? Jesus, his family, she thought. Had she done anything to provoke him? To lead him on? To that question she could positively say no. Or could she?

And so Angeline had sat, letting the sun warm her back as Neil busied himself around this beautiful suite. It really was just like a Princesses Castle, she thought. Angeline had always wanted to be a princess in a beautiful castle. Dad had promised her one when she was very little.

A knock at the door, polite, almost apologetic. Neil sprang to the door. A tall, slim young woman entered, with a smile.

"Just pop it on the table, there." offered Neil, as she entered, pushing a trolley, covered in white linen.

On the trolley sat a silver tray, a bottle of Champagne in a silver pewter ice bucket, two elegant flutes, and two small silver bowls.

These contained a selection of nuts. Neil thanked the young woman, held the door for her as she exited.

Angeline rose quickly from the sofa, and joined Neil at the table.

Neil made to open the Champagne but Angeline interjected. "Aren't you gonna shake it first?" Angeline had asked that in such earnest an manner that Neil was taken aback. The look on Neil's face put Angeline on the defensive.

"What now?" She backed away slightly, beginning to redden. "Have I committed a fatal faux pas?"

"No. Of course not." Neil stammered. "It's just that I'm too mean to let good Champagne go to waste."

Angeline saw the way out, and took it.

Neil went to shake the bottle, Angeline grabbed at it, and put her hands over his. They stood, frozen for seconds, and then she lifted her hands away. Neil acted swiftly. He popped the cork, a passable amount of fluid spurted out, and then he was tipping the frothy liquid into the flutes. He lifted a glass to Angeline. "M'lady." He offered.

"Thank you good sir." She responded, taking the flute.

They drank deeply, it was good. It took effect. They smiled, and sat at either end of the sofa.

Neil brandished a bowl of nuts, and Angeline took great delight in pushing her long slim fingers around the bowl, extracting only the peanuts.

They laughed, and commented on the view, on the elegance of the suite, on the fact that the Champagne had almost gone. And then, out of the blue, Angeline asked; "Seriously Neil. What are you going to do?"

Neil hadn't seen this coming, and was caught off guard by the gentleness of her tone. By her concern.

"What do you mean?" Neil was probing now. Uneasy.

"Well, you're going to have to go back to your family, your wife, aren't you?" This was not delivered as a question, more a fait a compli. Neil rose to the bait.

"No. I love you Angeline. Whether you want me or not I cannot go back. I can't live a lie". Angeline looked steadily at him. He had spoken quietly, but with such intensity that she believed him. Believed in him. This man who had given up everything for her, even though he didn't really know her.

She thought about the conversations they had shared, the times he had made her laugh, the times he had just sat, and listened. She thought about how thoughtful he had been, how complimentary, how sincere.

Angeline leaned forward and kissed him.   Fully. Passionately.

Angeline was trembling. For a second it didn't make sense, nothing made sense. And then it didn't matter.

They rose together, and Neil wrapped strong arms around her. She allowed herself to be drawn in. To feel. Love.

Neil led her to the bedroom by the hand, and sat her down. They kissed forever. Neil was lost inside himself, he didn't want this to end. Ever. This feeling. These feelings. Angeline gave herself, fully. She wanted, needed to be held. To feel, again. They removed each other's clothes, laughing but nervous.

Angeline was aware of the effect her flawless body had on him as he smothered her with his lips and hands, stroking and pulling, kissing and gently biting. He toyed with her hair, pulling and twisting it. He turned her over and over, feeling, loving her.

This was so different, thought Angeline, through the mist. She had been to bed with men before. Since Him. But not like this... This was worship.

She twisted round and locked her long legs around him, around his firm body. He pulled away from her kiss and looked down at her, at her eyes and mouth, her firm breasts and flat stomach…At her beauty, and her youth.

He realized, with a feeling of utter panic, that he wasn't hard. It was too much, he had become so immersed in her that his body couldn't cope. He had over thought the moment. He twisted away, seeking to hide his embarrassment, to find the spark that would ignite him. She noticed. She didn't have the experience to know how to react. Or not.

"Seriously?" Was all that came from her mouth. She grabbed him and pulled his hand down between her legs. She opened her thighs and let his fingers in. She guided him with her own fingers. He responded. You didn't expect that, did you? She thought as he delved further in, and then found her. He played and teased, and she directed him.

Suddenly he was on her, and then inside her. Angeline pushed him away, and climbed on top of him. She grabbed him and pushed down on him. Neil let out a low groan, and pushed up to meet her as she rode him, hard and fast. Within minutes he could feel himself building to climax, he grabbed her hips to slow her down but she arched over him, not looking at him, lost in another world. Just sex.

They came together. She shuddered above him, and pushed down as hard as she possibly could, wanting everything. He pulled down on her buttocks, wanting, needing to be inside her, part of her. She opened her eyes as he came, and letting out a guttural noise from deep within herself, collapsed on top of him.

He felt her shaking. Crying? No, Angeline was laughing, convulsed with laughter. He pulled her face up by her hair.

"What the fuck?" He asked, incredulous.

"Cum face." Her response. Between a shield of laughing. Neil laughed too. He remembered a silly flirtatious conversation they had had, weeks ago, where they had jokingly commented about how funny people looked at the moment of orgasm.

They lay on the bed together, his arm draped around her shoulder, stroking her long black hair. He marvelled at how she looked, framed against the ivory pillows and pure white Egyptian cotton sheets. In truth, he had never seen anything as beautiful as her. So this is love, entered his mind. And stayed.

After a while they made love. It was tender, and then wild, he wanted to stay with her, in her, forever. He concentrated on a bead of perspiration as it rolled down the nape of her neck, towards the valley between her firm white breasts. He came. That didn't work, he smiled to himself.

After a while they lay. They spoke, quietly, determined to hold on to this moment. And then they cried. It seemed natural. Real. And they held each other, protected from the world. For a time.

The afternoon was gone. They started to dress, in silence. Angeline went to the bathroom. When she came out the defence was back up.

"This doesn't change anything Neil. We always knew this was going to happen. Now we should let go. You have to go back to your wife." Her eyes were red.

Not now. Please. Not now. Neil couldn't, wouldn't let go. Not now.

Angeline shrugged, and pulled a hair brush from her shoulder bag. She stared at herself in the gold edged, floor length mirror as she brushed her hair. She looked as if she didn't care. Inside however, something gave way. Something died.

Jayne.

Looked at the text. Amy. Coming home tomorrow. xx. Jayne was lost in emotion. She so badly wanted to be with Amy. To hold her. To tell her everything. But also, she thought, this was not how it was meant to be. Surely, she argued with herself, surely parents are supposed to be the rock that the offspring come back to, surely the parents are supposed to provide the support, the solace, when things went wrong. Not the other way round. Deep down, however, Jayne knew that this was a fight she was losing, a battle against which she had no defence. So she let it wash over her, this sense of relief, this feeling that she could survive.

Jayne then curled back into a ball, on her favourite chair. And slept.

Neil.

Was making plans. He had decided that the promotion which had been dangled in front of him several times recently, was going to be his way out. His new fresh start. He would go to Italy, to Milan, and oversee the implementation of the massive new project, the opening of the company's first overseas factory. He had turned this opportunity down twice already, citing the need to be in England with his young family as they went through their education.

But, that was then. Now, he told himself, there was no valid reason why he should stay. He would take Angeline, of course, as his personal assistant, and then. And then.

Neil didn't dare think past that point. Neil decided to go to the senior management team. He would bulldoze them with his plans, his enthusiasm.

Angeline.

Didn't look at dad. Her head was gone.

Peter made all the right noises, offered her whatever meal she would like, tried to make her laugh, and finally, reluctantly, asked her if she was okay.

Angeline was tired, she needed space, quiet. Time. She looked at him. "I'm sorry dad, I'm just really tired. It's been great having you here, I miss you so much. We can go out somewhere nice next weekend yeah? And we can plan the holiday?" Angeline smothered her dad with kisses, hugged him like there was no tomorrow, and, kissing her mum on the forehead, went up to her room. Four messages, and her WhatsApp was flashing. Neil.

Angeline turned her phone off. What had she done today? Inside she knew. She knew that she had wanted to lose herself, to forget, to hurt, someone. Anyone. It had been Neil. Well, she told herself, he was no better than any other man. He was quite willing to cheat on his wife, his family. She told herself that Neil didn't love her. He was using her. Like all men did. He just had a bit more charm. He had caught her off guard.

Angeline decided to leave the company, immediately, and to have nothing more to do with Neil. He's old enough to be my dad, she said to herself, without conviction.

Neil.

Wondered if Angeline had lost her phone. He had been trying to reach her all evening, without success. He dismissed the idea of going round to her house. Awkward that, he thought. Instead he busied himself putting together a viable business plan for even more expansion abroad. With himself at the helm of course. He broke his golden rule, sitting on his bed in the hotel room at the edge of the motorway which was becoming home, tapping away on his laptop. Neil was immersed in his vision. Neil was happy.

Jayne.

Busied herself around the house. Amy would be home later that afternoon. Jayne would be meeting her at the airport at 14.50. Jayne was excited, and apprehensive. She really didn't know what she was going to say. She did feel, however, a palpable sense of relief, of escape. She would listen to Amy's take on things, and then would act, accordingly. After so long alone, Jayne was clutching at straws. She knew it, and resented it. But this wasn't her fault. This was Neil's doing. Jayne decided to go out and buy flowers for Amy's room.

Neil.

Shaved, showered, dressed and then headed off to work.

Still no answer from Angeline. Still, he thought, he would see her in work, maybe put his plans to her. Hear what she thought. Neil noticed how bright the day was. How warm. Reaching work he bounded up the steps, swiped in, and headed for his office. He sat down, and rang extension 6. "Hi Tony, it's Neil, yeah, hi, good thanks. Listen mate, could you do me a favour? When Angeline comes in could you get her to give me a bell? She's off? Oh. Okay. Thanks anyway. No it's nothing important. Yeah, cheers. Later."

Putting the phone down, Neil reflected. It would make sense for Angeline to have more than one day off if she was throwing a sickie. It would look more realistic. Neil put the thought to one side, and concentrated on a more important matter. Namely, getting that move abroad.

Jayne.

Was beginning to feel the anxiety in the pit of her stomach again. The plane, as all planes are in late summer, was late, two hours, and Jayne had been pacing up and down the same strip of carpet in the overcrowded arrival lounge for most of that two hours. She kept glancing up at the flickering screen hoping to see some change in the aircraft status, but, no, time was playing games. She had gone over and over in her mind about how to approach Amy, what she was going to say, how she was going to tell Amy that inside, she was falling apart. Jayne was acutely aware that, although she needed someone to understand, someone to take away these feelings, this dread, she didn't want to alarm her daughter, or put any undue pressure on her. Amy is eighteen years old, she found herself repeating, in her mind. Eighteen.

The flickering screen spluttered into life. "Thank God." She said. She looked around, at all the other people, waiting, expectant, happy. And the tears rolled down, unabashed.

Neil.

Decided to go home.

He needed to see Jayne, talk, if she would listen. He needed to wash clothes. He needed to eat.

The idea of returning to that empty room at the end of the motorway depressed him, especially after the previous day. Neil smiled to himself as he climbed into his car. He would text Angeline one more time, and if he still hadn't received any response by the time he passed her house, maybe he would swing by. It wouldn't seem very unusual that a work colleague, on their way home, might pop by to inquire about a colleague's health.

Neil knew this was absolute bollocks, but he really needed to see Angeline, to be near her. And, what the hell? He thought, surely she would appreciate his motives? In the back of his mind Neil recognized that this was probably not a wise course of action. But, he missed her, terribly, and had thought of nothing else but her, all day. He accelerated away from work.

Jayne.

Squeezed Amy so tightly that Amy had actually attempted to pull away.

"Ouch mum, not so hard." Joking, but serious. Amy held her mums hand as they headed for the car. She had got the earliest flight back. She had texted Jack, but Jack had replied that he was busy, and was going to stay busy.

Amy wasn't sure whether her brother was miffed that mum hadn't contacted him, or whether he just didn't want, or couldn't get involved. Either way, she was disappointed in him. Not for the first time.

Jayne helped Amy stow away her suitcase and backpack in the boot of the Citroen, and then they sped off, towards home.

Neil.

Changed his mind about an impromptu visit to Angeline's, mainly due to the fact he didn't actually know which of the large attractive houses she lived in, as he had only ever picked her up at the corner of her road, and partly also because an inner sense was telling him that it really wasn't a good idea.

He relaxed and drove to the house he used to call home. Upon arrival he found the house empty. He let himself in, and went up to run a bath.

Jayne.

Had ran out of things to say. Amy had sat next to her all the way home, hugging a small, beaded bag she had bought whilst travelling.

Occasionally Amy would flick a glance at her mum, seeing the tired, hollow eyes, and lines of doubt and age, around her mouth. And inside Amy wept, and grew angry. Amy was angry at herself, for not coming back sooner, and she was angry at Jack, for not caring, or being a coward. And she was angry most of all, at her dad.

Jayne's heart sank as she spotted Neil's car in the drive. She bumped slightly up the kerb in front of her house. Her house, not his. The thought flashed into her brain. Was this where it would all come to a head? Was this the end?

She dismissed the thought as she opened the door.

Neil.

Had heard the car arrive as he padded down the stairs, his arms full of towels and clothing. Jayne? He went to open the door for her, dropping clothing on the stairs. Too late, the door swung inwards and Neil saw firstly Jayne, and then Amy. He was completely taken aback. "Amy." He spluttered out, as Jayne, ignoring him, passed into the doorway. "Amy. I didn't know you were coming back now, I mean today. I... "

"You bastard." The response was like a bullet. The pain and anguish, and guilt, was spat at him in those two words. Amy pushed past him, red faced and tearful, and hurried into the house, following mum. Away from him.

Neil stood for a second, in the doorway, and then he closed the door, and, ignoring the spilled washing, went upstairs, finished dressing, and left.

Angeline.

Looked at her phone. It was time for a night out. She would see if the girls fancied a trek into town. She looked at the number of missed calls and texts. From Neil. Only one since midday though. Was he finally getting the message? Or not? as it were. She smiled at her weak joke, and then decided that she really wasn't in the mood for a night out. Not yet.

Neil.

Was stunned.   Angeline had handed in her notice...
Yesterday.

Neil had gone into work, determined to speak to her, to
let her know of his plans, his ambitions. For the pair of
them.   He hadn't tried to contact her the previous
evening. In the front of his mind he had reasoned that
she had needed a little time alone, after their time
together. In the back of his mind, however there had
been a nagging sensation. A doubt. He had pushed it
farther back, out of sight. But not out of mind. It
nestled next to Amy's reaction to him.

He had unsuccessfully tried to blot that out too. He had
decided to ignore anything he couldn't cope with.
Anything that hurt too much.

Neil realized he was coming towards a new beginning.
Or an ending. He retreated into something meaningful.
Safe?

He had spent the evening going over and over what he
was going to say, how he was going to convince the
company, and Angeline, that his business proposals
were sound, financially viable, and workable.. He had
gone to sleep that night full of ideas, and doubts. He

had dreamt of Angeline, and Amy, and war, and desolation. He had woken in fear, in the middle of the night. He couldn't bring details to mind, but the feeling, the dread enveloped him. The fear didn't leave.

Neil had gone to work that morning determined, and ready to fight, for whatever was left. He had spoken to Tony, briefly, on the phone. "Yes" he had confirmed, she had handed in her notice. With immediate effect.

She had given the requisite weeks' notice, but as she was still off sick, this had been waived. "No, she isn't expected to be back at all, sorry mate. Was it something important?" Tony had asked. Neil had thought for a long hard second before replying. "No. Nothing important." He said. "Nothing important." He crawled through the day, and at five thirty decided to go home. To the place he used to call home.

He had made no other plans. He had no plans at all, now.

Jayne.

Listened to Amy.

Amy who was trying to help, but didn't know the full story. Amy, who could not possibly feel the torment and sheer nausea that was a constant inside.

And Jayne yet again reproached herself for asking her daughter to come home, to listen, to make things right?

Jayne allowed herself a peep inside her own mind. She wondered where Neil was now. Was he with that... thing? Yes, thought Jayne, it was that things fault. Neil had been weak, she had led him on, and...And Jayne knew this wasn't true. Neil was not weak, or stupid. He had told Jayne that he loved that girl, that tall, beautiful young woman. He had meant it. Whatever Neil's version of love was, he obviously believed it.

That hurt Jayne even more. She closed her mind. It didn't feel quite as bad if she didn't have to think about it.

Jayne sat down next to Amy, kissed her on the forehead, smiled and said. "Don't you worry baby, it'll be all right."

Amy had ran out of things to say. She didn't have the life experience to console her mother. To help. To sort things out. She used the kiss to excuse herself. Amy went to her room, and tried to think.

Neil.

Stopped several times on his journey. On the way home he had seen the sign for the Belfry, and his heart had leapt. What was going on with Angeline? Inside he knew. Inside he knew everything was coming to an end. She was young and beautiful. She was avoiding him. She had left her job. Why on Earth would she want him? That thought had flitted in and out of his mind these last few hours.

What had happened at the Belfry made no sense, he thought, but then, in his world, as things stood, nothing did.

It was almost as if he was preparing himself for the worst. He could not, would not, admit it to himself, of course. That would have been too much for him to handle.

Neil's mind was in such tumult that he had pulled over and texted Angeline, again. And again. Neil was growing desperate. He had never felt like this. Ever.

He had seriously considered asking Human Resources for Angeline's address, then dismissed this as a flight of fancy. They would never release that sort of information, even if he could dream up a story that would have given him a legitimate reason for asking.

He thought about going to where Angeline lived, and knocking on every door of every one of the houses in that beautiful, secluded cul-de-sac. Until she came out. Not a good idea, either, he concluded. He had visions of trying to explain himself, to the Police.

And so Neil headed slowly, reluctantly, towards home. Towards?

Jayne.

Was startled by the sight of Neil coming through the door.

"Just passing through are you? Six thirty? Is it past her bedtime?" Jayne stood up and left the lounge. Neil followed her into the kitchen. "Where's Amy?" He asked. Jayne wheeled around. "Why? So you can upset her again? What do you want Amy for? Borrow her pram? I think we threw that away when she reached puberty Neil... and"

Neil interjected, "For Fucks sake Jayne. Angeline is twenty three and..." Jayne exploded. "I don't want to hear her name Neil, I don't care how fuckin old she is. I don't care if you love her. I don't care if you've fucked her into tomorrow, in a fucking crèche. I care about the fact that she has ruined my life Neil. Our lives. Mine, and the children, Neil. Your bloody children."

Neil stood, as Jayne turned away. She stared out of the kitchen window, onto the dry grass of the small, well-kept square of garden. It had been a long summer with only a little rain, the odd shower, yesterday? Or the day before? Neil stood, as her shoulders convulsed. She wouldn't let him see her cry.

Neil.

Neil stood, for a time, and then put his hands on Jayne's shoulders. He felt the tension, the stiffening. But she hadn't pulled away, or pushed his hands away. "Let go Neil." She had spoken, still not turning towards him. It was quiet. It wasn't angry. It wasn't an order.

Neil didn't know what to do. At that instant, in that silent kitchen, with his wife, his life partner, he didn't want to let go. He wanted to make it right. He wanted to make it all disappear. To end. He let go of Jayne's shoulders.

She continued to look out of the window.

Neil took a deep breath. "Jayne, I'm sorry, so sorry. I know what I've done. I do, really. I never ever wanted to hurt you. Or the kids." Neil sensed Jayne tensing, but carried on. "I know I can't make it right. But if you want I...I...I don't know. I just want this to stop, Jayne. I'm sorry." Neil had finished

He didn't know how to make it right, but he really did regret. Everything.

Jayne.

Listened to Neil. Heard him falter. Fail.

She thought of Amy, and Jack, and how she herself felt inside. The dark, dark place she was in. The knots in her stomach. The ache in her heart. And she surrendered.

Jayne turned and faced Neil. "So, what do you do now Neil? What will you do that makes everything better? Everything right."

It wasn't the response Neil had expected. He was taken aback. He floundered for an answer, took too long, and Jayne cut in.

"I really don't know what to do Neil. You have betrayed me, betrayed everything we stood for. You were supposed to be different Neil. We were in love for God's sake."

"I still love you Jayne. Of course I do. This wasn't planned. It was wrong. I was wrong. I am so sorry Jayne. Neil trailed off, conscious that Jayne's eyes were boring into him. Into his heart. His soul.

"So, you want to come back Neil? You want to make it right, make it work? The question inside the question unfolded, and Neil, desperate, dove in

"We can make it work Jayne. If you want it to." Jaynes eyes flashed, and she spat out; "But what about your little tart Neil?   Where is she in all this?

Neil looked evenly at Jayne. "She's gone.   Left the company. I don't know where she is. I don't care."

Jayne looked at him for a long time.   "Gone for good Neil? Gone for good? Jaynes mind was racing, trying to figure things out. She knew she could have forced the truth out of him. But she really wasn't sure she wanted to know. She hadn't expected any of this.

Neil turned away and sat down at the kitchen table. Jayne noticed how tired he looked. How old and tired.

"I'll put something on for dinner. You staying?" She asked.

Over the ensuing weeks a sliver of normality returned to Jayne's life. Neil moved back in, but was careful to find space, to disappear upstairs if he detected that Jayne or Amy were uncomfortable in his presence. It was quiet, but bearable.

Amy went to Bristol. Jayne and Neil bought stuff, and helped her pack, drove her there. It was quiet in the car, fragile. But Amy appeared to cope with it, and even hugged Neil briefly when he and Jayne were leaving.

Neil had wept silent tears then. Jayne had noticed this, and felt a strange feeling inside. A feeling she hadn't felt in a long time.

Jack came and went in a few days, seemingly indifferent to the atmosphere.

Jayne thought to herself, we're losing him. But Jack was growing up, she admitted. These things happen.

In the house together Jayne and Neil felt their way. Words were exchanged, safe words, sentences developed, and then even a stab at humour. Just a weak joke, or remembrance. But it was a start. A start.

13. 24. Thursday,
Ninth October.

Exactly eleven weeks to the day since Angeline had walked into Neil's office, Neil looked at his phone.

He only looked at his private mobile during lunch hour. There was seldom any messages for him. The green light pulsed, and Neil flicked open. Hey it's me. Could you meet me after work?

For a split second Neil thought the text had come from Jayne. She had recently taken to turning up to meet him after work, and she always messaged him beforehand. The text was from Angeline.

Neil froze. He read the text again. Checked the date, the time.

She had messaged him ten minutes ago. She would have been aware he was on his lunch.

Neil sat, looking at his phone.

Finally he sent one word. Why? In a flash the response. Yes or no? Yes. He replied instantly. Too late to think. Consider.

After a brief pause he typed in; 5.30? Gates?

Yes. The reply came instantly.

Neil stared at the phone, and panicked. What? Why? Why now?

Should he go or text back and say no, he wouldn't be there?

The afternoon swam around him, he didn't notice.

At 5.20 he logged off, tidied the desk, smiled at Rowena, yet another junior trouble shooter, she liked that title, and, grabbing his jacket, made his way downstairs.

Neil swiped out, and joined the queue down the steps.

He headed towards the double gates. At first he couldn't see her, the mesh of the gates and the throng of people milling around, hid her from view.

And then he could see her, standing tall, statuesque, a haughty expression on her face.   This was her self-defence.

Neil had forgotten how tall she was, nearly as tall as him, in her heels.

People glanced at her as they left the premises.

Angeline stood by the gates looking at him as he walked towards her.

She was wearing her black leather biker jacket, tight faded jeans and knee length suede boots. Her hair was tied in a bun, scraped away from her face. Her eyes were a heavy black, and her mouth a crimson sulky bow.

She looks, thought Neil, like she's just stepped out of a magazine, or a rock music video. She was everything he had ever desired. He had tried to forget her, about how he had felt about her. He loved her, wanted, needed her. It would never work, he told himself, again. He was, in that instant, back where it had all began.

Neil stood, inches from Angeline.

"Hello." He said, dying in front of her beauty.

"Hello." She replied. A silence, which Neil broke.

"I didn't expect to see you again."

Angeline looked steadily at Neil, and said. "I'm pregnant."